A DAY
TO
REMEM

FIONA PHILLIPS

ACCENT PRESS LTD

Published by Accent Press Ltd – 2007
ISBN 1905170904/9781905170906
Copyright © Fiona Phillips and Lynne Barrett-Lee 2007

The Quick Reads project in Wales is a joint venture between the Basic
Skills Agency and the Welsh Books Council. Titles are funded through
the Basic Skills Agency as part of the National Basic Skills Strategy for
Wales on behalf of the Welsh Assembly Government.

Printed and bound in the UK

Cover Design by Emma Barnes

CHAPTER ONE

They say bad news, like buses, always comes in threes. Had I thought about this, early, on that sunny June Saturday, I might just have stayed in bed.

But of course I didn't think about it. Nothing had happened yet. Instead, I was busy pulling open the curtains and yawning, and thinking how soaring summer temperatures and itchy uniforms don't mix, however nice the day would be for the bride.

If you're chauffeur to a bride, a uniform's a must. Because if a wedding's going to be a day to remember, all the little details have to be right. That's what my firm was called, A Day To Remember, and we provided special cars for special days out. Weddings, of course, but also birthdays and christenings. Whatever, as my ex-husband used to say, the clients wanted.

Today's Day To Remember was, as they often were, a wedding. Second marriage, quite small, in a hotel. Three hours work for me, tops, and then I could get home. But before that, I had to get up and get the wedding car ready. Get the ribbons tied on, get the champagne nicely chilled, and then get our elderly Rolls Royce round to the bride's house in plenty of time. So no time for a lie-in.

I padded off into the bathroom and turned on the shower, picking up stray items of Josh's clothing as I went. Teenage sons, I thought fondly, as I coiled up my hair and stuffed it into a shower cap – would I ever get him house trained? I really needed to remind him where the laundry basket was.

With the shower on at full blast, I didn't hear the phone. So the first I knew about the first bit of bad news was the sound of Josh's voice bellowing up the stairs.

'Mum? Mu-um!!'

I switched the shower off. 'Yes?'

'Rhys is on the phone.'

Rhys was a local farmer. We kept our two wedding cars in his barn.

'Coming!' I reached for a bath towel, still dripping. I trotted down the stairs and Josh handed me the phone.

'Lovely morning,' Rhys said. I agreed that it was. 'I was wondering,' he added, 'what you had on today. Only Tom's at a loose end and in need of some cash. You want him to go over the roller for you?'

Tom was Rhys's son, and was fifteen, like Josh. And also like Josh he liked to earn himself pocket-money by washing and polishing our two cars.

'Don't worry about the Rolls,' I said. 'Josh only did it on Thursday. But if he's keen to earn some money, he could give the limo a polish. We're not going to need it till next weekend, and it'll be one less job to do.'

The limo was our other car. We needed both when we had bigger jobs.

'OK,' said Rhys. 'I'll have him do that. When's it coming back?'

'Back? Back from where?'

'From wherever it is.'

'It's not there?'

'Nope.'

'Oh, well. I expect Steve's popped out to get the tyre pressures checked or something.'

Steve was the driver who worked for me part-time. I usually gave him all the evening jobs to do. I'd spent more than enough time over the years working nights. Also keeping two expensive cars on the road meant there was always something that needed doing. That was one reason I so looked forward to the time when they were gone from my life.

'I don't think so,' said Rhys. 'It's not been here since he took it on Friday morning.'

'Friday morning? It's been gone that long?'

This was strange. Where could he have taken it? As far as I knew it hadn't been used since a prom do last Tuesday, and Steve certainly hadn't said anything to me. 'That's odd,' I said. 'Are you sure it's not there?'

Rhys laughed his big laugh. 'Not unless it's sneaked off and hidden behind a haystack! No, I promise you, Jo, it isn't here.'

By the time I'd dressed and driven up to the farm to get the Rolls, I was mystified. What was going on? I'd tried Steve on both his mobile and his house phone, and failed to get him on either. What had he been doing taking the limo out on Friday morning? We definitely had had no bookings for Friday. I'd double checked. I was actively turning away work at the moment.

With only a month left in college (where I was training – very proudly – for my certificate in floristry) I was taking only a few new bookings till the autumn, when I was going to put the cars and the business up for sale and get on, finally, with the life I wanted to lead. But that was then and this was now, and my limo and my driver had both vanished.

Rhys was out in the yard giving the concrete a hose-down when I arrived. Tom was following with a broom. Time was getting on and I still had the ribbons to put on the car. I grabbed the roll of ribbon and the cool box from the back of my ancient Fiesta and locked it. It always felt a bit ridiculous to be stepping out of my battered old tin can and driving away in something so posh.

'Still no sign of it, I suppose?' I asked, as I made my way across the yard. Rhys shook his head.

'Nope.'

'And you've not seen anything of Steve? He's supposed to be working tonight.'

Rhys shook his head. 'Not since Friday morning, like I said, and I didn't really see him then. He just waved as he left. You not heard from him at all?'

No, I hadn't. But one thing was for sure. When I did he would have some explaining to do.

The bride wore ivory. A slinky, off-the-shoulder number with a tight boned bodice and a fishtail skirt, all of which made it something of a challenge for her to get in and out of the car. The groom sweltered in a morning coat and wobbly top hat, and looked like he'd rather be at home in front of the telly. If I ever got married a second time, I thought, I would wear something much more comfortable. Something simple and feminine and soft. Having attended my first wedding trussed up like Bo Peep, I was pretty much decided on that.

As was usual, I had an hour's wait between the ceremony and the photos, which they were having done on the beach down near Barry. I usually spent the time doing something useful. Sometimes reading a book, sometimes writing stuff for college. Or making shopping lists or making plans. Though sometimes, if the wedding was held at a church I didn't know, I spent much of it looking for a ladies' loo. And, more often than not, failing to find one.

Today, though, I sat in the car and fretted. Where on earth were Steve and the limo? If what Rhys had told me was true, this wasn't the first time he'd taken it without asking me. Could he have been involved in an accident? What if he was hurt? What if he was lying in a hospital bed, unable to call because he was unable to speak?

Once I'd taken the couple to Barry, I drove back to the farm mentally crossing my fingers.

Perhaps he'd be back now and all would be well.

But there was still no limo at the farm, and no word from Steve when I got home. No response either to the many messages I'd left him. I called him again, even so. If he didn't show soon, I would have to get the Rolls out again. We had an anniversary do booked for seven. A job which I'd already booked Steve for and which I'd now have to do myself.

Josh wasn't in, so I phoned him as well. As usual, he was on his skateboard at the skate park.

'Yo, Mum,' he said.

I told him I'd have to do the booking, which didn't bother him much. These things never did. He was much too busy having fun. 'But your tea,' I explained. 'I'll have to get it for you now. I'll have to leave before six.'

'I'm not hungry, Mum. I'll get myself something later.'

'Even so, I need to know you're home before I go.'

He sighed loudly. 'Mu-um! I'm fifteen!'

'Yes.' I sighed too. 'I'm well aware of that, Josh. But I can't go off to Cowbridge without knowing you're home safely.'

'I'll be fine. I'll get a lift. Hang on –'

I hung on, for some time. 'It's all right,' he said at last. 'I can get a lift off Owen's dad.'

'Are you *sure*?'

'Yes, I'm *sure*. Mum, *chill*. I'll be fine.'

Chill, indeed. If I did the amount of chilling Josh was always telling me to, I'd have to be stored in a deep freeze. But I did put him out of my mind. He was right. He'd be fine. He always was, wasn't he?

So much for a mother's intuition.

Two hours later, I'd delivered the anniversary couple to their party, put the Rolls back in the barn, and was just driving back down our road when my mobile rang. I still didn't think of Josh. I assumed that by now he'd be home. I thought it might be Steve, at long last. But no. It was someone else. Owen's father. Calling with my second bit of bad news...

CHAPTER TWO

'He's done *what?*'

I was still sitting in the car on the drive as I spoke, and there now seemed no point in getting out.

'Broken his arm, I think,' said Owen's dad, who was calling me from outside the accident and emergency department of the hospital. He'd driven Josh there and would now wait until I arrived. 'Doing some stunt or other,' he added. 'But it's nothing serious so don't worry. It's just that there's a bit of a wait, what with it being Saturday evening. Boys will be boys, eh?'

Hmm, I thought. And mothers will be mothers. I'd give him a hug, of course, and say 'there, there'. But then I'd give him a very large piece of my mind.

But in fact, I didn't, because Josh looked so sorry for himself when I got there. And also as if he was trying very hard not to cry. We waited, as predicted, for a good couple of hours. I spent some of this, in my motherly fashion, pointing out the importance of elbow and knee pads. Josh, in his fifteen-year-old fashion, reminded me that they wouldn't have stopped him breaking his arm.

As it turned out, it wasn't his arm but his wrist that was broken. A neat and clean break that would be easy to fix. They put it in plaster, which pleased Josh enormously, and then we were free to head home.

It was dark when we emerged from the A and E building, and a light rain had started falling. The sort of rain that looks harmless, but actually gets you very, very wet. Still, at least the day had cooled off a little. We hurried to the multi-storey car park and I shoved coins into the pay machine. By the time we were in the car, I was almost dropping with tiredness. I was very much looking forward to getting home, getting out of my uniform, eating something, opening some wine, and putting my feet up in front of the telly before anything else could happen.

But we'd just reached the bottom of the last exit ramp when my third bit of bad news showed up, with a totally unexpected, ear-splitting thump. The car that had been following us out of the car park had slammed straight – and very hard – into the back of my car.

I leapt out, as you do, almost refusing to believe my Saturday could have got any worse. Yet, seeing the damage, it clearly had. And how!

'Bloody hell!' observed Josh, who had got out as well.

'Language!' I snapped. But 'bloody hell' was right. We were both in a state of utter shock. The car behind – or, more correctly, the one now rammed up against my Fiesta – was a big blue Mercedes, and its owner, who was obviously even more shocked than we were, had not yet got out. In fact, he seemed to be involved in some sort of tussle inside. Was he having a fight with his seat belt?

One thing I did know was that if he wanted a fight I could give him one. I marched up and was just about to rap on the car window, when he all but exploded out of the driver's door. I jumped back, alarmed. He was a crazy man, clearly.

Just how crazy soon became clear, because he then started frantically tugging at his clothing. His shorts, to be exact, which were dusty and dirty, and which he promptly pulled down, shouting 'Ouch! Ow*ee!*' as he did so. Josh and I looked on, astonished, but he didn't seem to notice. Once the shorts were down – he

11

was wearing red boxers – he stamped his feet out of them, picked them up and shook them out. Then he made an inspection of the inside of his thigh, said 'bloody hell' and grabbed at something with his finger and thumb. Only then, finally, did he seem to notice our existence. The whole thing had taken mere seconds.

'I've been stung!' he announced. 'Look!' He thrust his hand out towards me. There was something tiny and black between his finger and thumb. The sting, I supposed. 'Look at the size of it! God, it's still pumping!' He threw it away in disgust.

Being in a dark empty car park with a man in his underpants isn't something I have much experience of, so at this point I was speechless. I was glad when Josh came around to my side of the car. He may have only been fifteen and with his right arm in plaster, but he was at least a foot taller than I was. The man then grabbed his shorts and started putting them on again, which was a relief.

'Um –' I began, feeling very slightly braver.

'Oh, God,' he said, before I could get another word out. 'Look what I've done to your car!'

He zipped up the shorts and went to inspect the damage. 'God,' he said again. 'I am so, so sorry. It all happened so quickly. Just – zing! It was like a red hot poker going into my leg. And then my foot must have slipped off the brake.' He rubbed again at his thigh, then squatted down to take a closer look.

I was beginning to feel bolder by now. 'And landed on the accelerator, judging by the way you slammed into us,' I noted crossly. 'Look at the state of my bumper!'

He winced again. 'Oh dear,' he said. 'What a mess. Oh, I am so, so sorry.'

He stood up again and pushed his hand through his hair. It was curly and longish and just a little on the scruffy side, and not at all like the sort of hair you'd expect to find on a man who was my sort of age and drove such a posh car. But then I guess the same might be said for me when I was working. Though not right now. My own car was worn out, exhausted, and very much the worse for wear, and so, I felt grimly, was I.

'I'm sorry,' he said again. 'Really. But I didn't *mean* to do it –'

'Even so, you have,' I said, ignoring the fact that he was rubbing his thigh again with a pained expression on his face.

'And I'll obviously pay for the damage and everything...'

We all turned then, hearing another car approach. It stopped at the top of the ramp.

'Look,' he said. 'We'd better get these cars out of the way, hadn't we? Then we can swap details and so on. Yes?' I nodded miserably. What else was there to do?

But my car being where it was (a couple of feet further forward than it had been before he hit it), I didn't have space to move it out of the way unless he reversed his up the ramp first. Josh and I got back into the car and waited, and before long heard the noise of his engine starting up. And seconds after that another noise. A tearing sound. Before we'd even turned to look, it was followed by another. A clatter this time, of something hitting the floor.

'Oh, God. What on earth was *that*?' I asked Josh.

He turned around to see. 'Not exactly sure, Mum. But something tells me it might well be your bumper.'

As any woman will tell you, there are times when a situation simply has to be taken in hand. This was one such, so I took prompt action. I immediately burst into tears.

'Don't cry, Mum,' said Josh, placing his

good hand on my shoulder and patting me a bit. 'It'll all be okay. You're just tired.'

This would normally have snapped me out of it. There's nothing that makes you smile quite as much as your children coming over all caring. But seeing the man with the Mercedes holding what was indeed my bumper, I felt less like smiling and more like ramming the thing up his nose. I shoved the car into reverse and moved it out of the way.

Still snivelling, I got out again. The Mercedes man had put the bumper out of the way and was now moving his own car. Which, I noted furiously, was hardly dented at all. He parked alongside us and got out once again.

'I'm so sorry,' he began as I clambered out.

'Don't you "sorry"' me!' I ranted, pointing at the bumper. 'What am I supposed to do now?'

'Oh, please don't cr –'

God, *men*. 'And don't you dare tell me not to cry!' I barked. 'I've had a pig of a day, I've been two hours in casualty getting my son's wrist put in plaster, and now my car is in pieces as well!'

He turned to Josh. 'Oh, I'm so sorry,' he said again, nodding towards Josh's arm. 'I didn't realise.'

All this apologising. Anyone would have thought he'd been personally responsible. But saying sorry wasn't going to get anything fixed, was it? I glared at him and tried to swallow the lump that was stuck in my throat. How ridiculous to burst into tears like that. He must think I was deranged.

He certainly looked at a loss to know what to do next, so I went and took cover behind my open car door, in case he decided he should apologise some more. I knew that, if he did, I'd start crying again. But some instinct seemed to tell him he shouldn't, and he turned back to Josh.

'How'd you do that, anyway?'

Josh seemed pleased to have found someone to tell about his stunt. Someone who wouldn't nag him about not being careful. Someone who might just be impressed. 'Doing an Ollie,' he said, with some pride. 'Got at least *this* much air though.' He spread his arms to demonstrate. 'And landed it too. It was just that this stupid kid on a BMX collided with me.'

'Ouch,' said the man, nodding like he knew just what Josh meant. 'Still, way to go! I used to be a bit of a skateboarder myself, as it happens. Do you know Tony Hawk? I met him once, you know.'

I didn't have a clue what they were talking about, though Josh was clearly quite excited by this news. I didn't give a fig who Tony bloody Hawk was, only that right now every man on the planet seemed intent on ruining my life. I pulled my handbag out of the car and started looking in it for a tissue to blow my nose with. And also a pen. I didn't want to be here all night.

By the time I'd done that, the man had already found some paper and a pen of his own and was busy bent over the bonnet of his car, presumably writing down his details. I pulled one of my business cards from my purse and added my home address and phone number on the back.

'Sign your plaster?' he asked Josh as I was writing.

Josh glanced at me to check and then nodded. 'Why not?' Clearly someone so up on skateboarding matters must command total respect. The man passed me his piece of paper, looking relieved that I'd stopped blubbing at last.

'There you are,' he said.

I read it. Matt Williams, his name was. Short for Matthew, I guessed. But he looked like a Matt. He looked like a skateboarding, surfing kind of Matt. Not at all like a man in a big blue Mercedes. Not wearing those scruffy shorts. He finished writing on Josh's plaster and I handed him my card.

' "*A Day To Remember*",' he read out from the front. 'Well,' he said, brightly, clearly keen to cheer me up. 'Whichever way you look at it, we've certainly had that!'

You don't know the half of it, I thought grimly.

CHAPTER THREE

'What you need,' said my sister Jan, the following morning, 'is a nice cup of tea. And then you can tell me all about it.'

A nice cup of tea was my sister's answer to everything. Well, everything that couldn't be solved by my 'finding a nice bloke' to take care of me, that is. I was grateful that this was just a cup-of-tea day. It could be wearing, having your little sister hassling you about men all the time. Especially when men were the cause of all your problems.

I sat down in her tidy kitchen and put my head on the table. The wood was cold and smooth and it occurred to me that what I needed was not a cup of tea but a bucket of iced water. So I could throw it over Steve's treacherous head. And Josh's. *And* the man with the Mercedes. Everyone. Every *man*.

My sister, whose life always seemed so much more peaceful than mine, had made me a cup of tea the day I told her my husband Carl had run off to Alicante with the lap dancer. Or, rather, THAT lap dancer, as we all took to calling her. Which was incorrect because she wasn't a lap dancer by then. She was the receptionist for A Day To Remember, of course. Funny how life works out.

Still, all that had happened two years ago, and I was much happier these days on my own. Though I wasn't happy right now. Why did everything have to go wrong all at once? Why couldn't troubles come one at a time?

I lifted my head from the table. Jan was at the sink, filling her peppermint green kettle. The room was full of the smell of roasting chicken. I'd forgotten the last time Josh and I had sat down to a proper Sunday lunch together. Roll on September and a chance to have our weekends back. 'I don't want a cup of tea, thanks,' I told her.

'A glass of wine, then?'

I shook my head a second time. She turned and glanced at her kitchen clock. It wasn't quite noon. 'Hmm,' she agreed. 'You're right. Bit early.'

'What I need,' I told her, counting with my fingers, 'is one driver, one limo and my car to be fixed. Oh, and Josh to finish his geography coursework. That'll do for now. Can you fix it?'

We both smiled. Then she came round the

table and sat down opposite me. 'This is all too complicated,' she said. 'Start at the beginning.'

So I started at the beginning with the limo and Steve disappearing, and finished with the case of the bee up the leg.

A bumble bee, it had been. A really big one, it turned out. The man had found it in the footwell and showed it to us. Josh, who'd been stung by a bee the previous summer, had felt very sorry for him. I hadn't. I was much too busy feeling sorry for myself.

'It's so *unfair*,' I said, with feeling. 'How unlucky can you get? Because if Steve hadn't run off with the car I wouldn't have had to do the job in the evening, would I?'

'I suppose not. '

'And if I hadn't had to do the job in the evening, Josh wouldn't have been running amok in the skate park as late as he was. And if Josh hadn't still been there he wouldn't have broken his wrist, would he? And if he hadn't broken his wrist, we wouldn't have had to go to the hospital, and if we hadn't been at the hospital, we wouldn't have been in the car park.'

'Fair point.'

'And if we hadn't been in the car park, I wouldn't have had my car bashed up. You know what? I'm going to kill Steve when I get my hands on him.'

Jan got up again and squeezed my arm before attending to her chicken. 'But are you sure it's him who's taken the limo?' she said, opening the oven door and letting a blast of heat out. 'Couldn't it have been stolen by someone else?'

'No. I don't think so. Rhys says Steve took it away Friday morning and he hasn't seen it since.' I thumped the table with the flat of my hand. 'And now it turns out he's been using it lots. Rhys told me. Moonlighting with it. How DARE he!'

'Well,' she said, closing the oven door again. 'I'm sure he'll be back with it before you know it.'

I frowned. 'I'm not sure I share your confidence about that.'

I'd never been sure about Steve. But when Carl left and I took over what was left of his business, I kept Steve on because it didn't seem fair to chuck him out of the job. It wasn't much, I knew – two days work a week, at most – but it added to the wages he earned from his day job. Whatever that was. It had never been clear. It wasn't even Steve himself that was the problem. He was generally reliable. It was just that he mixed with some less friendly types. The sort of people, in fact, that you wouldn't much want in the back of your limo. But perhaps Jan was right. Perhaps he and the limo would turn up again soon. I couldn't quite believe he would steal it.

'Well, whatever. The main thing is, what about *your* car? Is it very badly damaged?'

'I won't know till Monday evening, when the garage have inspected it. It looked like it was.'

'But he'll pay for it, of course.'

'He says so. I hope so. I've got to send him the estimate when I get it.'

Jan smiled. 'And what of the bee?'

'The bee,' I said grimly, 'has paid with its life.'

Poor little bee, I thought. And poor little me.

CHAPTER FOUR

Not that I felt sorry for myself on a regular basis. Not even on a Monday morning. Unlike most people I knew, I *liked* Mondays.

Since I'd started back at college last autumn, Mondays meant the future. The time when I'd be able to sell the cars and what was left of my ex's business, and start my new career. It wasn't the most highbrow of ambitions, but I'd always wanted to open my own flower shop, and keeping the business going for a while meant I could afford to go to college and get the qualifications I'd need.

I'd been working in a florists when I first met Carl, but his business was growing and it needed to be managed. And then we got married and had Josh and the years had flown by. Somehow my ambitions had flown with them. But now I was finally free and could do what I liked. Nothing was going to stop me.

Assuming, that was, I still had two cars to sell. There'd still been no word from Steve, and no answer from his phone, and the limo wasn't back in the barn. I'd checked.

Josh was feeling fine, though, and was keen to get to school and show off his battle scars. I wrote him a long note for his teacher explaining why he hadn't been able to complete his essay on Macbeth, and wondered if I could write one for myself to explain to my tutor why I hadn't managed to finish *my* essay, either.

I got the call from the garage just as I was coming through the front door on Monday evening. As I'd suspected, it was going to cost lots of money, but as it wasn't my money, I didn't much care. What I *did* care about, though, was that it wouldn't be fixed until Friday, which meant the rest of the week with no transport. Not unless I wanted to take myself off to college each day in an ancient Rolls Royce, which I didn't. Parked up there all day, I'd be lucky if it stayed intact.

I sighed, and found the number of the man from the car park. I dialled it. It was answered immediately, by a woman.

'Marie Williams.'

'Oh, hello,' I said. 'My name's Joanna Morgan. I'm calling about the repairs to my car. I was wondering if I could have a word with Mr Williams –'

'Oh, of course,' she said. She had a soft, sing-song voice. She sounded nice. His wife, I assumed. 'You must be the lady from the hospital,' she said pleasantly. 'Matt told me all about it. Dear me, what a disaster! I do hope you haven't been too inconvenienced. I'll just go and see if I can find him for you. Hang on a tic.'

I duly hung on, and a couple of minutes later, I could hear footsteps echoing as they approached the phone. I imagined what their house might look like. Probably went with their car. Elegant and grand. Parquet flooring, most probably. Obviously a big house. Much bigger than ours.

There was a clatter as he picked up the phone.

Except it wasn't him. It was his wife again. 'I'm so sorry,' she said. 'I thought he was in the garden. But he isn't. He's gone out. Can I take a message?'

So I gave her all the details, double checked their address and promised I'd have the garage post the estimate to them in the morning. Then I got back to finishing my essay and wondering, for at least the tenth time that day, where exactly my limo had got to.

CHAPTER FIVE

'You should call the police,' advised Jan, who'd called me for an update. 'You must. Because he's obviously nicked it.'

It was Tuesday evening, and I'd *still* not heard from Steve. I wasn't sure what to do. I'd thought about reporting it stolen all day Monday, but I still wasn't convinced it was the right thing to do. Something else, surely, must have happened. Something bad? And yet the car was registered in my name, so if there *had* been an accident, someone would have informed me by now, wouldn't they? Time was running out, however, and we had a two-car wedding at the weekend.

'I don't know,' I said. 'I still can't believe he would do that. He's lots of things, sure –'

'Like a no-good waster.'

'But not a thief. He wouldn't do that to me.'

'But someone else might have done.'

'I would have heard about it by now. From Steve. He would have told me *some*thing. And besides, Rhys told me the car's been out overnight before. More than once. So –'

'*What?* The cheek of it! You see? That just proves my point. He's been taking you for a ride. And now you have the evidence. You should have got rid of him the same time you got rid of that rat-fink ex-husband of yours.'

We'd been here before. Many, many times. One day Jan would realise that our marriage had been in trouble long before the lap-dancer went and sat in his. But if it made her feel better to cast him as the villain, there wasn't a great deal I could do. 'Let's not start on him, eh?' I said. 'That's all history now.'

I heard her exhale. 'Okay, okay,' she said. 'You're right. I'm sorry. But my point is still the same. You're too trusting, Jo. Too busy seeing the best in everyone. And then you get trampled on. I'm just trying to look out for you, that's all.'

Jan was right, of course. She generally is. Perhaps I *had* been too trusting with Steve. Perhaps I *was* too trusting, full stop. I promised her I'd call the police first thing in the morning, and then I got back to the more important business of college and my overdue essay.

I was just finishing it when the doorbell rang. I checked the time. It was after seven and I still hadn't started on dinner.

'Shall I get that, Mum?' asked Josh. He was sitting with me at the kitchen table doing his homework. Any excuse for a distraction.

'Don't worry,' I said, smiling. 'You stick at that. I'll go.'

I could make out a dark shape in the glass panel in the front door, and as I walked up the hallway I thought with a surge of relief that it was finally Steve with my limo. But the shape was too tall and altogether too slim. Unless Steve had been away at some secret diet camp, the person on the doorstep was somebody else.

It was. When I opened the door I didn't recognise the man at all. He was wearing a grey suit and a striped blue tie and was carrying a bunch of carnations, and a huge bar of chocolate. Perhaps he was going to try and sell me a kitchen or some PVC windows, and this was a wacky new sales ploy. But no. He thrust the bar of chocolate towards me. 'For your son,' he said, smiling sheepishly. 'How's his wrist?'

It took two more seconds before I worked out who he was. 'Oh!' I said, finally. 'You're the man from the hospital! Mr Williams!'

'It's Matt,' he said. 'Please. But yes. The very same.' He smiled. 'Oh, and these are for you.' He now thrust the flowers at me. 'By way of a proper apology.'

I let go of the front door and took them from him, a little flustered to find myself starting to blush. 'You didn't need to do that,' I told him. 'Really you didn't. But it's very kind of you, even so.'

I pushed the door out of the way with my elbow. He'd come all this way – his address, I'd already noticed, was in another, much grander, part of town – so the least I could do was invite him in.

He stepped over the doormat and stood a bit self-consciously in the hallway, filling it with the scent of expensive aftershave. His hair, I noticed then, was shorter and tidier than it had been, though not a lot shorter and not a lot tidier. And although the suave look did suit him, he still had the expression of a man who'd rather be wearing something else. I sniffed the carnations. They didn't smell at all. He clearly wasn't a man who knew much about flowers. Probably picked them up at a petrol station forecourt. But I didn't mind. It was a novelty for me, receiving flowers. From a man, that is. And such a nice one. Which made me instantly forgive him for ruining my week.

After all, it had been ruined already. By Steve.

'Did you get the estimate okay?' I asked

him. 'Oh, but you wouldn't have, of course. It was only posted this morning, so –'

'All sorted,' he said. 'I spoke to the garage first thing and had them fax it straight across to the insurers. Seemed more sensible. Speed things up a bit, at least. When are you getting it back?'

'Not till Friday,' I told him. He looked dismayed.

'That bad, then?'

'They had to order a new bumper from somewhere. And there's body work to do.'

He looked even more dismayed. 'God, that's a pain. The Merc only needed a touch up. Doesn't seem right, does it? Not when this whole thing has caused you so much hassle.'

He sounded like he meant it. How sweet of him, I thought. 'It is a very ancient old heap,' I reassured him. 'And don't worry,' I added brightly. 'I can manage on the bus.'

His brows shot up. 'The bus? They've not given you a courtesy car?' I shook my head. Bless him. What a different world he must live in. The nearest thing my trusty local garage could have offered was probably the owner's bicycle. The car itself wasn't worth a lot more.

'No,' I said, smiling. 'But, like I say, I'm fine on the bus.'

I don't know why I was carrying on like that. It wasn't fine at all. It was a hassle, as he'd said, for both me and for Josh. And despite my jolly tone, he obviously thought so too.

'Then you must phone them right away and get one. It'll all be covered by the insurance. The whole thing *was* my fault, after all – well, the bee's fault – ' He grinned. 'So I insist. Look, shall *I* call them and sort it out for you?'

'No, really,' I said again. That's the thing about me. Pride. Independence in all things. It's almost an instinct. 'I'll be fine.'

'Are you sure?'

I grinned back, to reassure him some more. 'Yes,' I said firmly. 'I'm *sure.*'

'But, look.' He shuffled from one foot to the other. 'The main reason I came was to say that if there's anything I can do to help – anything at *all* – you will let me know, won't you?'

I agreed that I would. I even offered him a coffee, but he had to get back. He was on his way home. So I thanked him for coming and sent him on his way and smiled at the thought that, for all the Steves and Carls in the world, there were actually some very nice men out there too. A married one, in this case, so off limits, sadly. Even if he hadn't been married, he was way out of my league. But at least it gave me hope, which was nice in itself.

Just a shame he couldn't magic my limo back for me. However, to do that, he'd have to have been a magician, and though he was actually quite magic to look at, he wasn't, I thought, the real thing.

CHAPTER SIX

In fact, no magic was required.

By Wednesday tea time, with no word from Steve, I'd decided I'd have to take action. Although I still felt sure he hadn't stolen the car, what else could I do but report it? I had the insurance to think about. But it couldn't have been more than half an hour after I'd put the phone down to the local police station, when I heard the doorbell.

I went out to answer it, and there on the step, *finally*, was my absentee driver, looking as though he'd just gone ten rounds with Mike Tyson, and lost.

They talk about black eyes, don't they? But Steve's eye – well, the skin around it, at any rate – certainly wasn't black. It was green and purple and yellow round the edges, and every other sort of colour a person's face shouldn't be. He also had a cut – held with a neat row of blue stitches – that curved in a line from his other cheek to his chin. I stood there, open mouthed, and gaped at him.

'Good God!' I said, feeling horribly guilty. I

shouldn't have called the police. He'd been hurt. But when? How? I gaped a bit more. 'What on earth's happened to *you*?'

He sort of grinned (Steve's always been one for grinning) but doing so must have hurt, because he stopped grinning and frowned. 'Spot of bother,' he said.

He'd always been a man of few words. I needed more. 'What sort of bother?'

He grimaced. 'Big sort of bother. Look, can I come in?'

I ushered him into the living room, anxious for answers.

'But where on earth have you *been*?' I asked, following him in and noting his weary walk. 'I've been worried sick!'

He sat down carefully on the edge of the sofa. 'Um, Birmingham.'

'Birmingham? What were you doing *there*?'

'Um,' he said again.

Um, indeed. It turned out that Steve *had* been moonlighting a bit lately, just as I'd thought. Not much, by all accounts, and he was very, very sorry. But he'd needed an extra few bob (I didn't ask what for) and as the limo was just sitting there in the barn, it had seemed crazy not to use it when there were so many jobs out there.

I didn't ask him why he hadn't asked me, because I already knew the answer. I would have said no. Since starting at college, I'd pretty much stopped dealing with that side of the limo business. We'd done plenty of evening work over the years, but once I was on my own, I really didn't want to work weeknights any more – I wanted to be there for Josh.

Neither did I want Steve, or anyone else, doing it. It made lots of money, but Stag and Hen parties often ended up with trouble. Sick, drunken passengers and all the problems they caused. When I came to sell the limo, which would be very soon now, I wanted it clean, and in one piece.

Steve knew all this, and had mostly respected my wishes up to now. I'd told him I'd recommend him to whoever bought the cars and the business.

But this time, he told me, he hadn't been able to resist. He'd taken a soon-to-be-married mate of his on a stag do. Him and seven friends. In *my* limo. And got involved in just the sort of brawl that had put me off those sort of jobs. Great.

'I'm sorry,' he said again. He reached into his jacket pocket and pulled out his wallet. 'I've been paid for the job and it's all yours, and – '

I waved it away. We could sort out money later. I just wanted to know what had happened. 'But why didn't you *call* me?'

'My mobile got smashed,' he said. 'And all my numbers were in it.'

Smashed. Even better. Just how bad had this fight been? 'I'm in the phone book,' I pointed out.

He shook his head. 'Not in Birmingham, you aren't.'

'Come *on*, Steve. You could have found my number if you'd wanted to. Ever heard of directory enquiries?'

He spread his hands and then rubbed one of them across his forehead. There was a cut on that too. He sighed. 'Look, the thing is, I was in hospital overnight –'

'I'm not surprised!'

'And then, well, I figured it wouldn't be a problem because I could get it all sorted and be back and everything and...erm...well...'

'Well, what?'

He looked sheepish.

'Well, without you noticing, I suppose.'

I blinked at him. 'Are you *mad*? How on earth did you think I wouldn't notice?'

'Well, the limo's not booked out till next weekend, so I thought maybe –'

'That I wouldn't spot that it wasn't actually there last Saturday?'

'You didn't need it last Saturday. I didn't think you'd worry –'

Which might have been true. If I'd simply not seen it, I would probably have thought he was off getting something on it fixed, just as I'd suggested to Rhys. If I hadn't spoken to Rhys and found out it had been absent overnight I might not have given it another thought. Not till I needed it, at any rate. Which had been on Saturday. What had he been *thinking*?

'But I did need you,' I pointed out. 'You were supposed to be doing a job for me on Saturday evening. Or had you forgotten?'

He looked confused for a few moments. Then he groaned. 'God. Yes. There was that late booking, wasn't there? The anniversary do.' He groaned again. 'Look, I'm sorry, Jo, but –'

I was becoming less sympathetic by the minute. 'Never mind about that,' I snapped, thinking he could groan all he liked. That was strictly *his* problem. I was busy with mine. 'So where's the car now?' I asked. 'Back in the barn?'

'Er, no. It's still in Birmingham,' he said.

CHAPTER SEVEN

This was all I needed. 'Still in *Birmingham*?'

'Er...yes,' said Steve. 'But don't worry.' He held up a hand, which I guess was supposed to reassure me. It didn't. 'It's being fixed up.'

'Fixed up? You mean the car's damaged too? Great. So just how bad is it, for God's sake?'

'Oh, nothing that can't be sorted.' I'll give him sorted, I thought. He shifted on the sofa and looked very uncomfortable. 'But that's the point. That's why I came. It's...er... going to take a bit longer than I thought.'

Oh, brilliant. 'How long?'

'About a week or so.'

'A *week* or so? *What?* But what about the wedding at the weekend? How am I supposed to do that with no limo?'

I was fuming by now. Forget the one black eye. I felt like giving him a pair.

But I didn't, because at that moment Josh came in. It would have set a bad example. Josh stood there and did a bit of gaping himself.

'Hello, mate,' said Steve, looking grateful for the diversion. He pointed to Josh's plaster.

'What happened to you, then?'

'Broke my wrist,' said Josh proudly. 'Skateboarding.' He pointed with his good arm. 'What happened to *you*?'

'Nothing he didn't deserve!' I snapped. I glared at Steve again. 'Not least because if you had been where you were supposed to be on Saturday night, that is, at work, Josh would have been where HE was supposed to be. That is, at home, and not doing loop-the-flipping-loops in the dark.'

'I wasn't doing loop-the-loops,' Josh said, looking pained. 'I told you. I was doing an Ollie. There's a difference.'

'But your wrist,' I pointed out, 'is broken just the same.'

'Anyway,' said Steve, rising. 'Think it's time I went.'

I stood up as well. 'And how exactly am I going to do this wedding on Saturday without a car?'

He jabbed a thumb towards his chest, obviously happier now he could say something positive. 'Don't worry. You've still got me. All you need to do is ask around, borrow some wheels, and we're sorted.'

I glared at him some more. I was fed up with people telling me things were sorted when they weren't. 'Oh, yeah, right,' I said. 'Just like that? In mid-June? And besides, do you honestly think I'm going to let you do it looking like that? You'd give the bridesmaids a fright.'

'Hmm,' he said, rubbing his face carefully. 'I hadn't thought of that.'

'You should take a look in the mirror,' I told him irritably. 'You look like you've just walked off the set of a slasher movie. Fine advert for us that would be.'

Though, I thought, if I never did another wedding I wouldn't care much. Including my own. I would definitely do that on foot. Not that there was much chance of that ever happening. You didn't meet a lot of men on the floristry course. Not ones that were interested in women, anyway. But I needed to get my limo back because selling it was vital to my future plans.

'Keep Saturday afternoon free anyway,' I told him. 'The way my luck's going this week, I might not have any choice.'

'Look,' he said again. 'I'm really, really sorry, Jo.'

And, as he stood there, I realised there was no point in ranting. It was done. He was back. Everything would get sorted. I was fully insured. And I did believe him when he said he was sorry.

Once he'd gone, I started making some calls. Though I knew it was going to be difficult, I'd surely find *someone* to do the job for me. I knew most of the other wedding car firms in Cardiff, and mostly we liked to help each other out.

By about the fifteenth phone call, however, I was beginning to feel much less charitable towards Steve. In fact, I was beginning to panic.

'Sorry, love,' said the latest on my list – an old friend of my ex's who ran a business like ours up in mid-Wales. 'But you know what it's like. It's June. You'd probably have more luck trying to borrow a jet plane right now.'

I thought I'd quite like to hire a jet plane. And a nice friendly pilot who'd take me away from Cardiff and plonk me down somewhere hot and sunny. A place where they didn't have cars. Or stag nights. Or weddings, come to that. It was one of the busiest wedding weekends in the calendar. He was right. Every car from here to Carmarthen would be booked.

I put down the phone and slapped shut my address book. 'God,' I said, sighing, to no-one in particular. 'What on earth am I going to *do*?'

Josh, who had been sitting at the table all

this time, working erratically on his geography coursework, put down his ruler and looked up.

'Mum,' he said. 'Why don't you just ask Auntie Jan?'

I shook my head. I'd already thought of my sister. 'Because she's going off on holiday on Saturday, remember? Besides, her muddy old 4x4 would hardly look the part, would it? This is a posh wedding, so it needs a posh car. That's what they've paid for so that's what I've got to find.'

'Oh, yeah,' he said. 'I hadn't thought about that.' He picked his ruler up again. Then he flapped it at me suddenly. 'I know! Why don't you ring that man and ask him?'

I drained my mug of cold coffee. 'What man?'

'The man from the hospital. You know. The bee man. The one who smashed up our car.'

I didn't understand. 'Him? Why ring *him*? What could *he* do?'

Bring me more flowers, maybe. That would be nice. No-one had bought me flowers in such a long time. I worked with them all day, but was never given them. And even if it was just a peace offering from nice, polite man, it was still, well, nice. I could see that by now Josh was looking at me in the way fifteen-year-old boys often look at their mothers. As if my brain was past its sell-by date. He was probably right.

'Durr, Mum. Ask him if you can borrow *his* car. He did say to let him know if there was anything he could do, didn't he?'

'*His* car?' I shook my head. 'Don't be silly.'

'What's silly about it? It's a big posh Mercedes. And he owes you one, doesn't he?'

That was true. But I shook my head again. 'No,' I said. 'You just can't ask to borrow complete strangers' cars. When he asked if there was anything he could do to help, I doubt *that* was what he had in mind.'

Josh shrugged. 'Whatever. Just a thought, that's all. When's tea ready, Mum? I'm starving.'

All through dinner, I thought about what Josh had said. And the more I thought about it, the more crazy it seemed. But when it got to nine-thirty and I'd run out of ideas, I wondered if maybe Josh was right. Mr Williams – Matt – had said he wanted to help. What harm could it do just to ask him? It might be a bit cheeky, but he *did* owe me one. And desperate problems called for desperate measures. Dare I call him? Yes, I thought. I must.

CHAPTER EIGHT

It took me till Thursday to pluck up the courage to make the call.

But a car was a car and I needed one badly. For less than three hours, that was all. All I'd need then was a driver and I could surely find a driver. If I couldn't, I'd just have to take some make-up along and have horror-movie Steve do it.

I called from college during our mid-morning break. Nothing ventured, nothing gained. He could only say no.

This time, he answered the phone himself. He sounded a bit out of breath.

'Mr Williams?' I could already feel myself blushing again. 'It's…er… Jo Morgan here. I'm so sorry to bother you, but –'

'Hello!' he said brightly. 'And, please, I told you, it's not Mr Williams. It's Matt.'

'Er…sorry. Matt.'

'That's better. So. What can I do for you?'

'Um, well, you know you said on Tuesday to let you know if there was anything you could do? Well, it's just that there is. I...er... wondered if I could ask you a favour?'

'Of course.'

Oh, this was just *so* embarrassing. I took a deep breath. 'Um, is there any chance I could borrow your car?'

'Borrow it? You mean you need a lift somewhere? When?'

'Um, not exactly a lift, as such. It's a little more complicated than that.'

And so I told him. I explained about the missing limo, and Steve's troubles in Birmingham and about the problem I had with the wedding on Saturday. And how I'd tried absolutely everywhere to find another limo. And how I'd failed. How Josh had reminded me that he'd said how anxious he had been to make amends after the accident and also that he had exactly the right kind of car. And how it wouldn't be any problem because I could find a driver and make the additions to our insurance and how I promised I'd get it back to him in one piece. By the time I'd finished speaking I was out of breath.

He laughed. A big booming laugh. 'Your life,' he remarked, once he'd finally finished laughing, 'sounds more dramatic than an episode of *EastEnders*!'

'It certainly feels like that at the moment,' I admitted. 'And I know it's a terrible cheek to ask you, but I've got to the point where I don't know quite who else *to* ask.'

'Well,' he answered, with encouraging brightness. 'I'm very glad you did. Saturday, you say? Can't see any problem with that. I guess I'd better double-check the insurance situation, but –'

'Oh, of course,' I said quickly. 'Yes, fine.'

'But I can't see why not. Hey, you can borrow me as well, if you like.'

'Oh, no. Don't worry. I'm sure I'll be able to find a driver from somewhere.'

'Hmm,' he said. 'Doesn't sound that likely, from what you've been saying. In any case, better if I drive it, don't you think? Less complicated all round.'

I blushed again. 'Oh, I couldn't possibly ask you –'

'Unless, of course, there's an unexpected outbreak of killer bees.'

I laughed myself, then. 'I'm sure there won't be. But look, are you absolutely sure? This feels like a terrible cheek –'

'It isn't,' he said firmly. 'I have nothing on on Saturday except grouting and tiling. All of which is getting very boring and can wait.'

I wasn't sure what his wife would have to say about that. Which made me feel even more guilty about it. What on earth had possessed me?

Necessity, I thought. So I mustn't be silly. 'One thing,' I said. 'Do you have a clean licence?'

Another booming laugh came down the phone line to my ear. 'Difficult for you to believe, I know,' he said. 'But incredibly, yes. Yes, I do.'

'Wow,' said Jan. 'That's amazing!' She gave me a hug. 'Oh, you're *so* clever!'

My sister and her family were off to Pembroke on holiday shortly, so she'd come over to leave me her house keys so I could feed her cats and her hamsters and her goldfish and her plants, hopefully without killing off too many of them. She'd also come to take me to college.

It was Friday, and the day of my final presentation. The huge period floral arrangement I'd designed for it wasn't something I could easily take on the bus. Not without causing a public nuisance and possibly gouging out a few eyes.

I picked it up carefully and walked slowly

towards the open front door.

'I don't know about that,' I said wryly. 'Knackered, for sure. I was up till two this morning creating this.'

Jan held the door for me then followed me down the path to her car. 'But you've got everything sorted? With Steve and the limo and the wedding booking and everything?'

I waited while she opened the back door of the car and shunted a pile of coats, boots and blankets out of the way. 'In a manner of speaking,' I said. 'We still don't have the limo back, and Steve looks like something out of the Addams family, so he's no use to me. But, yes, as it happens, I have.'

I put the arrangement very carefully on the seat, and did the seatbelt up around it. By now, I was feeling pretty pleased with myself about the whole thing. Matt had rung back and confirmed that he was okay for Saturday, I'd arranged the insurance and telephoned the bride to explain.

She didn't mind in the least that the white limo had been replaced by a metallic blue Mercedes. Be more of a squeeze for the bridesmaids, but would go so much better with her colour scheme. Thank heavens for practical clients, I thought. In the stressed world of weddings, there were few of them around.

I filled Jan in on the details. 'So everything's okay,' I finished, as we climbed in ourselves and set off for college. 'All I have to do is dig out a chauffeur's cap for him, and we're done. Steve's is probably in a gutter somewhere.'

'Ah, yes, Steve,' she said, adopting her "time to give you a lecture" tone of voice. 'What's going to happen about him?'

'Nothing,' I said. 'He's going to do all the bookings I have left in the diary and then I guess we'll go our separate ways.'

'And that's it?'

'That's it. He's offered to pay me for the bookings he did, and assuming the car comes back in the same state as it was when he took it, I'm happy with that.'

I had, by now, spoken to both the police and our insurers. Everything was covered and that was all that mattered. If the insurers wanted to sue any of Steve's passengers, that was their business. It wasn't my problem. In fact, I felt happily problem-free at the moment. I would be getting my own car back at the end of the day, I had two weeks left in college, and only another dozen bookings. Then, in

September, I could start realising my dreams. Some of them, anyway, which was good enough for now.

But Jan, like most sisters, could sometimes read my mind. 'And what about this knight in shining armour of yours? Matt, was it? Any action on that front?'

Typical. A bloke couldn't come within ten yards of me, without Jan thinking he might be the man of my dreams. Not that I didn't have the same dreams as any other divorced woman – that one day I'd meet someone lovely and live happily ever after – but I wasn't in the same rush as she was about it. I'd been out on a couple of dates after the divorce, but it was still early days. When the right man – or, okay, dashing knight – came along, I was convinced that I'd know it. Till then I was happy to bide my time.

So, yes, she might well be right. Matt might be a very nice man. But one not on my radar.

'No,' I said firmly. 'No action whatsoever.'

'Ah, you say that,' she said, in a tone that suggested she had forgotten who was the big sister. 'But you never know when or where Cupid's going to strike.'

Cupid, indeed. What planet was she on? 'I already *told* you, Jan. He's married.'

She looked disappointed. 'No, you didn't.'
'Yes, I *did*.'

CHAPTER NINE

There are all sorts of weddings. Big weddings, small weddings, grand weddings, cheap weddings. There are as many kinds of wedding as there different types of people. Though divorces, sadly, usually end up the same.

Saturday's wedding was a medium-sized wedding, unremarkable in almost every way except, as sometimes happens, that it was themed. Funny business, I always thought, giving a wedding a theme. Shouldn't the theme be simply 'happy ever after'? Wasn't that enough? But if that was what made them happy, so be it. Having been present at so many weddings over the years, there was little I hadn't already seen and been aghast at, so if it pleased the bride to style herself on the Little Mermaid, as this one had, then who was I to pass judgement? I just hoped, as I always did at weddings, that theirs would last.

'Unbelievable!' muttered Matt, nudging me as the bridal procession – in various shades of bright blue and green – had got themselves into formation for a couple of quick photos before we left for the church. Even the bride's father's suit was a nasty shade of turquoise. 'What's *that* all about?'

I leaned in a little closer so I wouldn't be overheard. 'I believe the groom is a scuba diving champion, or something. She told me they met on a reef.'

'On a reef?'

'In the sea. If I remember right, she was in a snorkling group on some package holiday outing and he whisked her off to show her...well,' I shrugged, stifling a giggle. 'Some fish, I suppose.'

It was a big church, one I'd been to many times before, so I knew where to find the loo, at least. It also had sufficient room that we could park both the cars off the road, which meant we didn't have to scoot off to some backstreet car park to wait, and could enjoy the sunshine from a bench in the churchyard.

It had already been a busy day. I'd had to get up, shower, get Josh off to some skateboarding event (for him to watch, not compete in – anything to get his fix) and then go over to the barn to check over and pick up the Rolls. After that, I'd had to find my way to Matt's house, which was every bit as grand and imposing as I'd expected. (What did he do for a living, I found myself wondering? I really knew so little about him.) It made more sense to go to him than him come to me because it was closer to where the bride lived. We'd then had to decorate both cars with the blue ribbons she'd ordered and get over to her house in plenty of time for her to decide that she didn't like the blue after all and could she have green ones instead?

'So this is what you do full time, then, is it?' Matt asked, once we'd parked the cars and were heading across the churchyard to wait. 'Provide cars for weddings and so on? Seems an unusual job for a woman.' He winked. 'If you don't mind me saying so, that is.'

'Not at all,' I replied, as we made our way across to the bench, which was sited beneath a large, spreading cedar tree. The shade was a relief. It was getting very hot. Another day to be wearing something other than a suit. Oh, for a day off!

We sat down. 'And you're right,' I added. 'I only know of one other firm that's run by a woman, so, yes, I am a bit of an oddity. But it's only temporary.' I explained about it having been my ex's business, and about my *real* career plans.

'And at least I won't have to spend any more weekends hanging around graveyards,' I observed. 'I'm beginning to feel like one of the undead.' I stretched my legs out in front of me and sighed. 'God, it's warm, isn't it? What I wouldn't give, right now, to be by a river somewhere. Sun sparkling on the water, chilled glass of wine, tartan blanket, some swans...'

'Swans?'

I smiled wistfully. I had lots of time, in my job, to think about all the things I'd rather be doing. 'Oh, ignore me,' I said. 'It's just a little picture I keep in my mind. A few swans floating past. A dozing fisherman on the riverbank. A good book. Some strawberries. Possibly a few bees...'

'Hmm,' he said. 'You can keep the bees. But the rest sounds pretty good. Mind you,' he said, stretching out a little himself now, crossing his long legs and linking his hands behind his head. 'Sitting here isn't so bad, either. Beats grouting, for sure.'

I wasn't sure what he meant, but then I remembered. 'Of course. Your tiling. Decorating, eh?'

'Putting in a new bathroom,' he said. Which I realised would explain his dusty scruffiness the first time I saw him. 'Well, I'm supposed to be. No matter. I shall crack on tomorrow.'

I felt guilty then, reminded that I really had no business invading his weekend. I sat up straight and turned towards him. 'I really am very grateful for your help today,' I said. I thought about the work that was waiting for him at home. 'Are you sure your wife doesn't mind?'

He looked confused for a moment. Then, suddenly, he grinned. 'I doubt she'd care much either way. As far as I know, she's in Melbourne.'

Now it was my turn to look shocked. 'Melbourne? Oh. Has she gone there for a holiday?' She might have, after all. I hadn't seen her when I'd called that morning.

He grinned again. 'Sort of, I suppose. Pretty long one, though. She's been there two years now and to my knowledge she hasn't got any plans to come back. Not to me, at any rate.'

'Two years?' I took this in. 'It wasn't your wife I spoke to on the phone, then?'

He tipped his head back and let out another of his big booming laughs. 'Oh, that is rich!' he said. I didn't know what was so funny. But something obviously was.

'Good Lord, no!' he said. 'Marie? Perish the thought. Actually, no. I shouldn't have said that. She's lovely. But also fifty-three and my sister-in-law. I don't have a wife. Just an ex-wife. I'm divorced.'

I thought about Jan's comment. And smiled to myself. 'Now I *am* confused,' I said, feeling quite jolly all of a sudden. 'So you're living with your sister-in-law?

He nodded. 'But only temporarily. I've been staying at my brother's for a few weeks. I'm kind of between jobs, between homes. And as he's out of action right now, I'm paying my way by putting in –'

'*Their* bathroom. I *see*.' It was beginning to make sense. It was *all* starting to make more sense. A nice kind of sense. And then I had a thought. 'You say your brother is out of action? How out of action?'

'He broke his ankle a few weeks back. Had to have a plate put in his leg. He's just had the op to remove it again. That was why I was at the hospital last weekend.' He grinned and spread his arms. 'And now I'm here! Funny how fate works sometimes, isn't it?'

I was just thinking that myself (and my thoughts were pretty pleasant ones) when I became aware that Matt was suddenly not looking at me any more. Instead, his attention was now on the distant church door. I stood up, and saw one of the bridesmaids staggering out. Which, only ten minutes into the service, definitely shouldn't be happening 'Uh-oh,' I said, with a familiar sinking feeling.

When you've attended as many weddings as I have, you see all sorts, believe me. The bridesmaid, who looked about twenty and was clutching her stomach, was being followed outside by a middle-aged lady, wearing a duck-egg blue, Mother of the Bride outfit.

She could have been the mother of the groom, of course. Either way, she was looking very stressed. Matt stood up too, and we hurried back across the churchyard.

'Something wrong?' I called as we approached. 'Can I help?'

The older woman looked very pleased to see me. The bridesmaid just looked grey.

'Do you have a phone?' the older woman asked breathily. 'I think we might need an ambulance.'

'An ambulance?' said Matt. 'What on earth's happened?'

The woman was about to tell us, but the bridesmaid got in first.

59

'I'm about to have a baby, that's what!' she yelled. Or at least that's what it sounded like. It was difficult to tell because she was almost doubled up, and talking mostly to her dress.

'No, you're *not*,' said the woman firmly. She turned to me. 'She's only twenty-two weeks.' She shook her head. 'Oh, dear. I do hope...' She looked worried for a moment, but then seemed determined to try and keep calm. 'You're *not*,' she said again, rubbing the girl's back. Her daughter, I guessed. 'You've just become overheated, that's all. Calm *down*, love. Deep breaths. That's it.'

'I'm telling you, Mum, I am – ooohhhh! Oh, God! Ooohhh –'

She was beginning to buckle, so I grabbed her from the other side. 'There's a bench. Come on. Over this way. Let's get you sitting down.'

'I'll call the ambulance, shall I?' Matt already had his phone out.

'Best you do, dear,' the woman said. 'And do you have any water?'

'We do,' I said. 'Matt? It's in the Rolls. Inside the cool box.' I fished in my jacket pocket and threw him my keys.

The girl was boiling to the touch. And it was clear that the situation wasn't helped by the tight bodice of her dress.

'Oh, my stomach...' she groaned, doubled over once again with pain, as we half dragged, half carried her over to the bench. I felt behind her and began to unfasten the buttons on the back. There were about twenty of them, fiddly and difficult to undo. Her mother, meanwhile, kept up a stream of bracing words. 'That's it, love. Deep breath. Come on. *In*. That's it. *Out*. And then *in*, and then *out*...'

Matt was by now loping across the grass again towards us, nimbly jumping gravestones as he ran. He looked a bit like a curly-haired James Bond.

'The ambulance is on its way,' he said. He held a bottle out. 'And here's the water.'

The mother took it from him and began unscrewing the top.

'Thanks so much. And we'd better get hold of Danny, hadn't we?'

I took the top from her. 'Danny?'

She nodded towards her daughter. 'My son-in-law.'

Matt looked back towards the church. 'He's not here?'

'He should have been. But he's a policeman. He was called in this morning –'

'Uuuugrhh!!!' went the bridesmaid. She flopped back against the bench, groaning

61

loudly. 'I think –' she gasped. 'Uurgh... I'm...uurgh... going to faint.'

We gently pushed her forward and put her head between her knees. She'd only been there a second or so when suddenly she struggled, and then sprang up again. 'No, I'm not,' she moaned. 'Oh, God. I'm going to be sick.'

And then she was. All over me.

CHAPTER TEN

I thought she looked a bit off-colour in the car,'
Matt said, as we watched the wedding party re-
assemble to start the service all over again.
They'd been lucky. The next wedding wasn't
scheduled till four, so they still had just enough
time to fit theirs in.

The ambulance had been and gone. Indeed,
by the time it had arrived, the bridesmaid,
having dumped her entire wedding breakfast
on me, had already announced that she felt
much better. Not better enough to do her duty
as a bridesmaid, but well enough that her
husband could stay at work and that her sister
could get married as planned. She watched
from the safe distance of a pew near the back.
Someone had even found her a bucket, just in
case.

A stomach upset, they'd announced, when
they'd examined her. Either that, or a bad bout
of late morning sickness, made worse by the
heat and the tightness of the dress. She'd been
suffering from it all through the pregnancy,
apparently, which made me feel sorry for her.

I'd suffered like that, too. But no problems with the baby, which, the paramedics said confidently, was *not* on its way. She just needed plenty of fluids and – once home – lots of rest, and a visit to the clinic on Monday.

'Lucky you, then,' I observed to Matt, looking down at – and smelling – my damp and crumpled suit. I'd got most of it off, but, boy, how the smell lingered. 'After all,' I said. 'She *could* have chucked up all over your car.'

But it was me who'd been lucky, I thought, even as I said this. Had she thrown up in the car, it would have been me who'd have had to pay for the cleaning. Which would have cost a lot more than my suit.

Matt took off his chauffeur's cap and ran a hand through his curls. 'Hey, you know that river?' he said. His eyes glittered with amusement.

'What about it?' I asked.

'Bet you'd quite like to jump in it now, eh?'

With everyone safely back in the church, there was nothing to be done now but wait, as before. There wasn't time for me to go home and get changed, so we went back to another bench – a dry one this time.

Matt loosened his tie a little and flopped

down on the seat. 'This sort of thing happen a lot, does it?'

I positioned myself at the far end of the bench where the sun could help dry my skirt. I smiled ruefully. 'Not this, exactly. But I've seen my fair share of dramas. Fainting – that's common. Punch-ups between parents. People falling out over where they've been sat. Even had a heart attack once –'

'Really?'

'An elderly guest. He lived to tell the tale, but then the marriage never happened. The groom decided he should take it as an omen.'

Matt laughed. 'Maybe he was right!'

I looked back towards the church. 'Well, I'm glad this one *is* happening. Though it's going to make us late getting back now –'

'Oh, don't worry about that. I've nothing to rush back for. Well, nothing I want to rush back for, at any rate. I can get back to work in the morning.'

'Is that what you do, then?' I asked him. 'Plumbing?'

He shook his head. 'God, no. I mean, I can tile and grout and graft with the best of them. But only under instruction. I'm probably not safe left alone with a wrench. No. Nothing like that. I'm a website designer. I only get my hands dirty on high days and holidays. The rest of the time I'm pretty much glued to a computer screen.' He pulled a face. 'Pretty boring, huh?'

'Not at all,' I said. 'That sounds interesting.' *He* sounded interesting. More interesting by the minute. Good-looking, charming, and now clever as well. '*Really*. I've never met a website designer before.'

'Don't you have a website for your business? You should.'

I smiled. 'So my son is always telling me. I did think about it a while back. But there doesn't seem much point when I'm selling it so soon.'

'For your flower shop, then. You should have one for that. What are you going to call it?'

'Sweet Peas.'

'Peas? For a flower shop?'

I rolled my eyes. 'Sweet Peas are flowers,' I said.

'Really?' He looked surprised. Not clever at *every*thing, then. But then he was a man. 'Well,' he said, 'you learn something new every day, don't you? And look, if you'd like me to play around with some ideas for you, I'd be happy to.'

So would I, I thought. But then I had another thought. 'You said you were between jobs. You've got a new one now, have you?'

'I have,' he said, looking pretty pleased about it. 'I'm off to the States in a couple of weeks. Can't wait.'

The States. In two weeks. Of *course*. That was why he was between homes as well. 'A new job?'

'A great job. Been looking for a job like this for a long time. Could lead to all sorts of exciting things.'

He was right. You do learn something new every day. Two things, on some days.

I'd finally found a man who did something other than let me down or wind me up. And he was leaving the country. How unlucky could you get?

CHAPTER ELEVEN

There wasn't much time to talk after that. By the time I'd got the champagne ready for the bride and groom (and more water on hand for the bilious bridesmaid) the service was over and it was time for the photos, a lot of which were due to be taken with the Rolls. After that it was a short (and, in my case, very smelly) ride to the reception, but as I'd put the roof down, it was bearable.

We parted at the hotel where the reception was being held, me to return the Rolls to its barn and Matt to get back to his tiling. By this time, the heat had become stickier than ever, and a mass of dark clouds was rolling towards us across the sky.

'Don't forget what I said, will you?' he said as he helped me put the roof up. I was in a hurry to get it done because rain was already starting to fall. It was the sort of rain that comes down in drops the size of sugar lumps, and feels about as heavy. At least it would soon be cooler.

'About what?' I asked.

'You know. About the website.'

I secured the last latch on the Rolls, then followed him across to help him take the ribbons off his car. I looked at him wistfully. I'd done some thinking on the way to the reception, mostly about it being bloody typical that just as I'd begun to feel properly interested in someone, they were zooming off to the other side of the world. Fate could be cruel.

But perhaps fate was right. Wouldn't do to get hung up over someone when I had so much else going on in my life.

'Thanks,' I said. 'That's kind of you. I won't.'

He looked at me from across the bonnet. 'I mean it. If you'd like me to come by some time next week and run through some templates with you before I go – no charge, of course – '

I started to nod. What would be nicer than to spend more time with him? Even if I wasn't sure what a template might be. And it *was* a good idea. I *would* want a website. I had to move with the times. But the human heart is sometimes cleverer than the head is, and makes you stop and think before you risk getting hurt.

'Oh, don't worry,' I said briskly. 'That's still a while away. I haven't even sold this business yet!' I undid the last bow at the top of the car door, and began rolling ribbon round my hand. 'And I wouldn't want to tempt fate by getting ahead of myself, would I?'

Quite, I thought. Quite. Given that I'd probably never see him again.

He came round to my side of the car with his own roll of ribbon. It was beginning to get spattered with rain. 'Fair enough,' he said. He looked disappointed, and I felt guilty again. After all, he didn't know that I fancied the pants off him. And he was just trying to be helpful. He shrugged. 'Just a thought.'

'Thank you.'

'If you change your mind – '

I nodded. 'Thanks. But, well, I'm going to be in college all week, and I've got to get Josh off to his father's. And with my driver still looking so grim, there's going to be a couple of evening jobs I'm going to have to do, and there's another wedding at the weekend –'

'Phew,' he said. 'Hold up. I'm getting worn out just listening. Jo, do you *ever* take a day off?'

'Not often, at the moment,' I admitted.

He took my hand in his and put the ribbon in my palm. Then closed his fingers over mine. 'Well, you *should*.'

CHAPTER TWELVE

Most of the time, cleaning cars was my least favourite chore, which wasn't surprising, given that I'd spent most of my adult life working in a business where cars had to be cleaned as carefully – and almost as often – as teeth. Cleaning cars gave you backache and arm ache and soggy skin, and also broke all your nails.

I'd set aside the following Wednesday afternoon to make some last minute changes to my college project and, if I finished it, go and see a movie with some college friends. But, instead, I was cleaning the Rolls, and, strangely, not minding at all. It was good to be busy. To get out of the house and do something physical.

I was cleaning the Rolls because Rhys's son Tom was unwell. He'd been tucked up in bed with a tummy bug since the weekend. Hmm, I thought. It must be spreading. I must keep my distance if I saw him. I'd had quite enough sick for one week.

Tom was supposed to have been cleaning the car because Josh was away doing work experience, and had opted, very sensibly, to do it with his dad. Why slog in a shop or an office in Cardiff if you could wangle a week at your dad's place in Spain?

I was pleased for him. He didn't see enough of his father. But I missed him. Must get out more, I thought. Must get the Rolls cleaned and go out with my mates. Must, in short, get a life. Jan was right. For far too long I'd been using work to hide myself away from the world. Time to get out there and join it again. It might be years before another man like Matt came along – but I'd hate to miss him if he did.

What I did almost miss was the sound of my phone. I'd left it in my bag in the Fiesta, and what with my singing – I always sang when cleaning cars – I didn't hear it in time to find it before it stopped. Luckily, however, it started again.

I found it and answered. Perhaps it was Josh, calling to let me know how he was getting on. But it wasn't. It was Matt. The hairs on the back of my neck began to prickle.

'You sound puffed out,' he remarked. 'Not interrupting anything, am I?'

I dropped the sponge into the bucket and wiped my other hand on my jeans. 'Not really,' I said, feeling a small flight of butterflies dance in my stomach. 'Nothing I'm in a rush to get back to, at any rate.'

Oh, my, I thought. Too late. I'm quoting him now. Boy, I really had got it bad.

'Good,' he said firmly. 'And I'm glad I've caught you, because I wanted a word. *I'm* the one in need of a favour now.'

'Oh,' I said, leaning back against the car. 'Okay. Right.'

'It's just that I'm leaving for the States next week and I wanted to do something for my brother and sister-in-law before I go. As a thank you for putting up with me these past few weeks.'

I wasn't sure where this was going, but then, *he* was going, so it didn't matter, did it? 'Oh, right,' I said again. 'Yes. Yes, you would do.'

'And of course I didn't know *what*, exactly. But then I had a brainwave. It's their anniversary at the weekend, you see. Twenty-fifth.'

'That's nice.'

'So I thought of you.'

'Me?'

'Yes, you.'

'Why me?'

'Have a guess.'

73

I couldn't think. 'I don't know.'

'You know what? I think you *are* better out of that business. I thought I'd arrange them a Day To Remember, of course!'

Why hadn't that occurred to me? Probably because my mind was somewhere else altogether. 'Oh, right,' I said. 'Of *course*. Silly me. Good idea.'

'So. Can you do it?'

'Do what?'

'Make yourself available at the weekend.'

'Um...well... I don't know. When, exactly? I have another wedding on Saturday –'

'Sunday, then,' he said. 'I was thinking Sunday would be best, actually. So are you free on Sunday? I know it's short notice, but if you haven't got anything else on...'

Bang went yet another day off. But then, he *had* done me a pretty big favour. Mustn't forget that. And it *was* nice to talk to him again. Tingle-at-the-back-of-the-neck nice. I pushed the thought away. 'No, no,' I said. 'Sunday's fine. Within reason. What sort of thing did you have in mind for them?'

'Not sure about the details yet, but something nice. Something special.'

'An evening do of some sort? Theatre? Only I can't be out late because my son's coming home then. Though I could certainly *take* them somewhere. No prob –'

'Oh, no. I wasn't thinking that. An evening hardly counts as a Day To Remember, does it? No, I was thinking an outing of some sort. Tell you what, how about we work on setting off some time in the morning?'

'We? You mean you're planning to go *with* them?'

'God, no. Wouldn't be much of an anniversary do with me tagging along, would it? No, no. I was just thinking about timings.'

'Of course. Well, you can let me know about that once you've decided what they're going to be doing, can't you? And how long you're going to want me and so on, yes?'

'No, no. No need. Tell you what, how about eleven?'

'Okay. Eleven at your – sorry, *their* house. With the Rolls?'

He laughed. 'You make it sound like something from a game of Cluedo. But, no. That won't work. I'll have to come to you first.'

'Why?'

'With the present. And…um…the balloons.'

'Balloons?'

'Yes. That'll work. I'll come to you, and we

can go and sort the car out and then we can both go round and fetch them and then you can take them off for their surprise.'

'Um…right.'

'Whatever that turns out to be. But that's sorted then, is it? That I come to you at, let me see… ten?'

'If you say so.'

'Excellent. Then I'll see you on Sunday.'

'Did you want ribbons?'

'Ribbons?'

'For the Rolls. Only I'm low on supplies, so if you wanted a certain colour –'

'No, no,' he said. 'Don't you worry about that. You can leave all the details to me.'

CHAPTER THIRTEEN

Why was it, I wondered, as I ironed my blouse on Sunday morning, that the sun always shone on days I was working, and hid behind the clouds whenever I got a day off?

Not that it mattered. It felt such a long time since I'd had a day to myself that if I got one I wouldn't care about the weather. Probably spend most of it catching up on sleep.

No time to rest now, though. Time was getting on. Matt would be here with his balloons in twenty minutes. Wouldn't look right to answer the door in my shorts. This, after all, was work.

When the doorbell rang five minutes later, I thought it must be my next door neighbour. He often stopped by on his way to church, to see if I wanted a Sunday paper from the shops on his way home. And I was still in my shorts.

'Surprise!!'

I didn't know who was saying this to me because the head was completely hidden by the largest bunch of sweet peas I had ever seen. There must have been hundreds, in shades of white and pink and lilac. Their scent was so powerful it almost knocked me off my feet.

The head appeared to one side. 'Oh, it's you, Matt!'

'The very same.'

'Gosh, you're early!' I took a step back and ushered him past me and inside. He was wearing shorts, too. The surfing shorts he'd had on when I'd first met him. Obviously a day off for him, at least. Either that, or a tiling and grouting day. The scent of the sweet peas filled the hall.

I felt flustered. 'I'm not ready yet. Er...as you can see. But I'll be as quick as I can.'

He stood there beaming at me, looking gorgeous, and I eyed the flowers carefully, trying to get my mind back in business-mode. 'Are those in any water?' I asked him. 'Because if they're not, they ought to be. They won't last the day otherwise.'

He inspected the bottom of the bouquet. 'Um, let me see. I think so.' He jiggled it about. 'Yes. Hear that? Sploshing. So, yes, I think they are.'

I took a look myself. 'Yes, you're right. That's okay then.' I began walking towards the kitchen to get my blouse. He followed. 'You'll have to give me ten minutes,' I said as we got there, 'to get changed into my uniform and sort my hair out and so on. If you want to make yourself a coffee, that's fine. The kettle's over there, and... What? What's so funny?'

He was standing in the middle of the kitchen and grinning. The same grin he'd been wearing the previous Saturday. '*What*?' I said again. 'What *is* it?'

He looked me up and down. I must have looked a fright. Hair all over the place, raggedy vest, faded shorts, and my favourite pair of flip flops, which were very, very old. I felt my cheeks begin to redden.

'You look perfect,' he said.

I blinked at him. 'What?'

'More than perfect. I know you can't strictly *be* more than perfect, but let's not be picky.' He was still holding the flowers, and he suddenly seemed to notice. 'And that blush,' he announced, 'goes very well with these.'

He held them out to me now.

'You mean those are for *me*?'

'Of course they're for you. My, you're slow on the uptake.'

I took them from him and our eyes met as I did so. My heart started thumping. Hearts might be clever but they're also unruly. I looked away. I hadn't felt this way in such a long time, and the feeling was so strong I didn't know what to do. My mouth was dry so I licked my lips. 'But what about your sister-in-law?'

'Marie?' He shook his head. 'Not into flowers. Gets asthma if you so much as put her outside.'

Oh,' I said, pushing my nose deep into the blooms, and not knowing what to say next. Except for thank you. So I said that.

'You're welcome,' he said. 'I'm glad you like them.'

'I *love* them. They're my favourites.'

'I know,' he said.

'How?'

'How do you think?' He grinned some more. 'Let's call it an educated guess.'

I put the flowers carefully on the table. 'But I still have to get ready,' I said, remembering what I was supposed to be doing. 'Time's getting on.'

He crossed the space between us. 'I told you, you don't need to. You look perfect as you are.'

'Your brother might not think so.'

'My brother won't be seeing you.'

'*What*?'

'Because we're not *going* to my brother's.'

I blinked. The tingle in the back of my neck was starting up again. 'We?'

'As in you and I. Seems to me you almost never make any time for yourself. Not willingly, anyway. So I thought I'd do something about it. Trick you into it, in fact. I'm going to take you out for a Day To Remember. Well, I hope I am. If you agree, that is.' He placed his hands on his hips. 'In fact, I'm not leaving till you do. '

I was so stunned I forgot about forgetting all about him. How could I when he was standing just inches from my nose? He was close enough to touch. Close enough to remind me that it had been a very long time since the closeness of a male person had had such a powerful effect on me. I'd also forgotten how scary that feeling was.

I tried to pull myself together. 'But what about their anniversary?'

'Oh, that's not till next month. And it's already sorted. Got them two tickets for the cricket. Much more their thing.' He held up some fingers. 'Well, three, in fact. I got one for myself while I was at it.'

It took several seconds for this to sink in. But then it did. 'For yourself? But won't you be in America?'

He shook his head. 'Not unless I lose my ticket home. Or get attacked by a swarm of

Yankee killer bees and get banged up in hospital or something.'

'But your new job –'

'What about it? Be long finished by then.'

'*Finished*? But –'

'How long do you think it takes to set up a website? I know it's going to be a pretty big website, but –'

My mouth was hanging open. 'So it's not a permanent job, then?'

He looked surprised. 'Course it isn't. Doesn't work like that.'

'It doesn't?'

He shook his head. 'I work for myself, same as you do. You do weddings – and flowers – and I do websites. Once you've done one you go off and do another one. That's how it works.'

'I never realised...'

'So I'll be in the States three, four weeks at the most.' He laughed. 'I'm not emigrating or anything!'

CHAPTER FOURTEEN

I was smiling inside so much by now that it couldn't help but show on my face. How stupid could a girl *be*?

Too stupid for words. But Matt didn't need to know that. 'Oh, I *see*,' I said, trying to look like it didn't much matter either way. 'I just assumed you were, well, moving out, moving on...'

'Oh, I am doing that,' he said. 'I'm in the middle of buying a flat down in Cardiff Bay.'

'Really?'

'Really.' He was still standing much too close for comfort. I took half a step back so I could breathe a little easier. He looked into my eyes. 'Which means I won't be far away. Which means that if I can prise you out of here sometime today and show you a good enough time, I'm hoping there'll be a chance we can do it all again.' He took half a step forward again as he said this. 'If you want to, that is.'

I stayed still this time, because I quite forgot to move. Our eyes met again. His were brown. Melted-chocolate brown. But it was me that was melting. 'What sort of good time?' I asked him.

He lifted his hands and began touching his fingers. 'Got the river, got the swans, got the blanket, got the wine. Got the strawberries and bees even, and that's despite the risk to my health. And –' he looked out of the window – 'pretty sure I've got the sun sparkling on the water as well. Still working on the fisherman. Have to keep our fingers crossed about him, I guess.'

'Wow,' I said. I meant it. I could live without the fisherman. No-one had *ever* done anything like this for me before. I was stunned. And completely stuck for words.

He lowered his hands and looked intently at me now. 'One Day To Remember, as ordered,' he said softly. 'Now all I need is a yes.'

Which is normally the point where the hero and heroine gaze deeply into each other's eyes and then move in for the closing kiss. But this being real life, just as we were about to do so, the phone started ringing. And it was nowhere to be seen.

I found it in the end, in Josh's bedroom. It was Steve.

When I got back downstairs, Matt was

looking out of the kitchen window. The curls on the back of his neck were like commas. Or a neat row of question marks, which had all now been answered. He turned around when he heard me.

'Everything okay?'

I glanced down at the scrap of paper in my hand. On it was jotted an important phone number. 'Yup,' I said. 'I'll just pop this somewhere safe.' I smiled as I stuck it to my cork board. Suddenly, the fortnight I'd decided to forget had turned, as if by magic, into something wonderful. 'That was Steve,' I said. 'My driver. He's bringing my limo back from Birmingham tomorrow, and it turns out he's got a definite buyer. For the Rolls as well. Isn't that great?'

'It is,' Matt agreed. 'You've forgiven him, then?'

'Actually,' I said, crossing the room in three strides, 'I think I should thank him, don't you?'

Matt's arms were there to greet me. So were his lips. And for five perfect minutes I forgot where I was. There was nothing in the world that could have prised us apart.

'And not *just* Steve,' I said, when we came up for air. He looped his arms around my waist. I put mine around his neck.

85

'Who, then?'

I shook my head and smiled. 'It's not a *who*,' I said. 'It's a lost limousine, a broken wrist and a bee sting.'

I kissed him again. And then I kissed him a third time. Sometimes things that come in threes are rather good...

BRING IT BACK HOME

BY NIALL GRIFFITHS

ISBN 1905170912 / 9781905170913
price £1.99

Chased by a hit-man, a young man returns home from London to a small town in Wales. Reconciliation with his family is alternated with his pursuer's progress. A long criminal connection is revealed but can he escape the sins of his fathers?

This is a tense, tightly written drama that will captivate the reader with fast, gut-wrenching action.

THE RUBBER WOMAN

BY LINDSAY ASHFORD

ISBN 1905170882 / 9781905170883

price £1.99

The world of Cardiff's sex trade hits the headlines when a woman is butchered and left for dead. Pauline distributes condoms to the women of the red light district and is known locally as 'the rubber woman'. She and Megan, a forensic psychologist, make it their mission to stop more women becoming victims. They don't know it yet, but one of them is already marked out for death.

AIM HIGH

BY DAME TANNI GREY THOMPSON

ISBN 1905170890 / 9781905170890
price £1.99

Aim High reveals what has motivated Dame Tanni Grey Thompson, UK's leading wheelchair athlete, through the highs and lows of her outstanding career. Her triumphs, which include winning 16 medals, eleven of which are gold, countless European titles, six London Marathons and over 30 world records have catapulted this Welsh wheelchair athlete firmly into the public consciousness.

THE CORPSE'S TALE

BY KATHERINE JOHN

ISBN 1905170319 / 9781905170319
price £2.99

Dai Morgan has the body of a man and the mind of a child. He lived with his mother in the Mid Wales village of Llan, next door to bright, beautiful 19 year old Anna Harris. The vicar found Anna's naked, battered body in the churchyard one morning. The police discovered Anna's bloodstained earring in Dai's pocket.

The judge gave Dai life.

After ten years in gaol Dai appealed against his sentence and was freed. Sergeants Trevor Joseph and Peter Collins are sent to Llan to reopen the case. But the villagers refuse to believe Dai innocent. The Llan police do not make mistakes or allow murderers to walk free.

Do they?

SECRETS

BY LYNNE BARRETT-LEE

ISBN 1905170300 / 9781905170302
price £2.99

Sisters Megan and Ffion have never had secrets, so when Megan goes to flat-sit all she's expecting is a rest and a change.

When a stranger called Jack phones, Megan wonders who he is. Ffion behaves like she's just seen a ghost, and refuses to say any more.

So is Jack a ghost? Ffion's not telling and when she disappears too, and the mystery deepens. Megan begins to fear for the future. She's always been the one who's looked after her little sister. Is this going to be the one time she can't?